Beatrice

More
Moves In

Alison Hughes

illustrated by Helen Flook

orca Echoes

ORCA BOOK PUBLISHERS

Library and Archives Canada Cataloguing in Publication

Hughes, Alison, 1966–, author
Beatrice More moves in / Alison Hughes ; illustrated by Helen Flook.
(Orca echoes)

Issued in print and electronic formats.
ISBN 978-1-4598-0761-7 (pbk.).—ISBN 978-1-4598-0762-4 (pdf).—
ISBN 978-1-4598-0763-1 (epub)

I. Flook, Helen, illustrator II. Title. III. Series: Orca echoes
PS8615.U3165B43 2015   jc813'.6   C2015-901726-2
C2015-901727-0

First published in the United States, 2015
Library of Congress Control Number: 2015935531

Summary: Beatrice struggles to manage her hopelessly disorganized family in an effort to make
a professional start in her new neighborhood in this early chapter book.

Orca Book Publishers gratefully acknowledges the support for its publishing programs
provided by the following agencies: the Government of Canada through the Canada Book Fund
and the Canada Council for the Arts, and the Province of British Columbia
through the BC Arts Council and the Book Publishing Tax Credit.

Cover artwork and interior illustrations by Helen Flook
Author photo by Barbara Heintzman

ORCA BOOK PUBLISHERS
www.orcabook.com

Printed and bound in Canada.

18   17   16   15   •   4   3   2   1

For my sisters,
Maureen and Jen

Chapter One

It wasn't that Beatrice More didn't like boxes. She did.

She especially liked boxes that were perfect squares. They stacked easily. They held things that would otherwise mess up the house. They were neat and tidy.

But today Beatrice was sick of boxes. Very, *very* sick of boxes. Looking around her new house, all she could see were stacks of them. On the floor. On the kitchen counters. On the furniture.

Boxes everywhere.

Beatrice had tried to tell the movers where to put the boxes. But they just carried them in and dumped them anywhere.

She tried to scrub off the smudgy, sticky handprints the movers left on the walls. But they kept making them faster than she could scrub them off.

She said, "Somebody's walking through the house *with their shoes on!*" very loudly several times before her mother finally shushed her.

The moving guys were horrible listeners. They just smiled, carried in more boxes with their sticky hands and kept making a bigger and bigger mess.

But the movers were gone now. The big, noisy moving truck was just pulling away from the driveway.

"It's about time," grumbled Beatrice. She stood in the living room with her hands on her hips. As she looked around, her eyes narrowed.

"What a *dump*," she said to herself, shaking her head slowly.

Her mother came into the room. She looked around happily.

"Well, this is exciting!" she said. "A new house, a new neighborhood, a new city! Are you excited, Bee?"

"*Beatrice.*" How many times had she told her family not to call her Bee? Nine thousand? Nineteen thousand? Ninety thousand? Bee was not a name at all. It was a letter. Or worse, an insect. An insect that buzzed annoyingly. An insect people ran away from, screaming.

Bee certainly wasn't the name of a future Olympic gymnastics gold-medal winner.

Or a future prize-winning scientist. Or a famous artist or writer. And those were all on Beatrice's list of *Very Successful Careers to Consider*.

"Have you *looked* at this place, Mom?" Beatrice said. "It's a mess! There are way, *way* too many boxes!"

"Well, Bee," said her mother, pushing her frizzy hair out of her eyes, "we only moved in this morning! We're just getting started."

Beatrice crossed her arms.

"I've already unpacked *my* room. Perfectly."

It was the first room she had all to herself. The first room she didn't have to share with her messy little sister, Sophie. Beatrice loved her new room. It was perfect.

"Wow. Really?" Her mother looked impressed. "Want to show me?"

On the door to Beatrice's room there was a small, square sign with neat purple letters.

Perfectly Mess-Free Zone
Grubby People: Go Away!

"Ah, here's your room," said her mother, smiling at the sign. She looked down at her grubby hands and rubbed them on her jeans.

"Now, if I let you in, you can't touch anything," warned Beatrice. "Nothing.

You can't wrinkle the bed or rumple the carpet or touch anything *at all*."

"Got it. I won't even breathe."

Beatrice opened the door.

The purple quilt on the bed was perfectly smooth. Not one wrinkle or ripple. The pillow was perfectly plumped. A square purple-and-white rug sat exactly in the center of the room.

The small white desk was perfectly clean. All of Beatrice's lists were stacked neatly in the top drawer. Each book in the bookcase had a special place—tallest to shortest. The stuffed animals on the bed were lined up alphabetically, from Annabelle (a duck) to Zeke (a horse).

"Well, you're right, Bee," sighed her mother. "It's perfect. But don't you want it to look a little lived-in? Maybe a little *less* perfect?"

Beatrice wasn't listening.

"Check out my closet," Beatrice said. She swung open the door. "Ta-daaaah!"

Beatrice's closet was, if possible, even neater than the rest of the room.

"Note the matching purple hangers," she said, "and the way I've hung all the clothes by color—blue, red, white, yellow and, of course, my favorite color, purple."

Her mother leaned against the door-jamb.

"How on earth do you live in the rest of our house?" she asked softly, shaking her head.

Beatrice didn't hear her. She was carefully shutting her closet door.

"Well, kiddo, your room looks great. Perfect, in fact," her mom said. "I guess I better start on the rest of this house.

Why don't you see how Sophie's doing with her new room?"

"Good idea," Beatrice said.

Her little sister should have unpacked at least *some* of her boxes by now. But Beatrice didn't expect much. Sophie was only four years old, after all. Four years younger than Beatrice.

Beatrice looked over at Sophie's room. There was a torn scrap of paper taped crookedly to the door.

Sophie had taped the paper to the door first, then written on it. The long tail of the *y* went down off the paper onto the white door.

Beatrice licked her finger and scrubbed at the smudge on the door. And scrubbed. And scrubbed. It didn't come off.

"Permanent marker," Beatrice said through gritted teeth. She made a mental

note to include Sophie's door on her list of *Things That Are Annoyingly Hard to Clean*.

She sighed and knocked at the door.

"Sophie? Are you in there? Are you all right?"

There was a muffled giggle and some shuffly sounds. Beatrice tried to open the door. It opened a tiny bit, then stopped.

It was stuck.

Stuck, Beatrice thought grimly, *in a huge pile of Sophie-mess.*

Chapter Two

Beatrice pushed and pushed at the door. It opened just a little bit more. Enough for her to squeeze her arm through.

She waved her arm into the room.

"Sophie, SOPHIE! The door's stuck!"

Beatrice heard a crash and more muffled giggling and shuffling.

Well, she's alive, Beatrice thought. *She's hopelessly messy, but she's alive.*

Beatrice pushed at the door. She opened and closed it. She pushed some more.

She backed up a few steps, then ran at the door. She thumped it hard with her shoulder.

More giggles from inside the room.

"I'm trying to *rescue* you, Sophie!" shouted Beatrice, rubbing her shoulder.

Inch by inch, Beatrice pushed the door. And inch by inch, the mess on the other side of the door moved back. Finally, there was just enough room, if Beatrice sucked in her breath very hard, for her to slide in sideways.

"This better not mess up my ponytail," Beatrice said.

She kicked away the boxes that had fallen in front of the door, opened the door wide and looked around.

Her heart sank. The room was a complete disaster. There were mountains of toys. There were piles of clothes.

There were heaps of stuffed animals. There were empty boxes littering the floor.

Beatrice crossed her arms.

Her left eye twitched.

This family is hopeless, she thought. *We've only been in our new house for a few hours, and it's already a dump.*

"Sophie? Where are you?" called Beatrice sharply.

"Dat you, Bee? I'm unner here!" called Sophie.

Beatrice turned and tripped over a half-unrolled carpet. She got up and stubbed her toe hard against a plastic bin of toys.

"*Ahhhhh!*" she cried. She hopped on one foot and rubbed her toe.

"Here I am!" shrieked Sophie, throwing back the blanket on the bed. She sat up with a huge smile on her

face. Some of her curly red hair stuck to her face. The rest of it stood straight up from her head in a bushy mess.

"Aha, there you are," said Beatrice, trying to smooth and pat down Sophie's hair. It wouldn't go down. It never did. *SOPHIE'S HAIR* was in capital letters on Beatrice's list of *Things I Cannot Control (But Wish I Could)*. The list also included *Time*, *The ocean* and *The smell in our car*.

Beatrice slid a hand over her own brown hair, relieved to find her ponytail was as neat as ever. Her hair was *much* neater than Sophie's, but there were waves in it, which annoyed her. She wanted perfectly straight hair. So Beatrice brushed her hair a lot, one hundred brush strokes every night.

"What have you been doing, Sophie?" Beatrice asked.

"Me an' my toys been playing BIG FORT! Mrs. Cow don't like it though."

She held out a crabby-looking baby doll. Mrs. Cow was Sophie's favorite toy.

"Doesn't. Mrs. Cow *doesn't* like it," corrected Beatrice.

"Right. A 'cause of the darknest," said Sophie in a dramatic whisper behind her hand.

"*Be*cause of the dark*ness*," said Beatrice. She looked at the scowling doll. "Why do you call her Mrs. Cow, Sophie? She's not actually a cow."

"A 'cause she's *married* to *Mr. Cow*, a 'course!" Sophie laughed and pointed to a large, smiling, stuffed yellow rabbit. Mr. Cow did not seem to be aware of his cranky doll-wife.

Beatrice closed her eyes.

"Okay. Whatever. Sophie, why haven't you put anything away? Your room's a total mess," she said. "Need some help?"

"It's all done!" said Sophie happily.

Beatrice stared at Sophie. "You're going to *leave* it this way?"

"Yup. I *love* it like this."

"But all the boxes..." protested Beatrice.

"I *play* in 'em."

"Your books..." Beatrice looked over to the corner where a box of books had been dumped on the floor in a fluttery heap, like an odd little book-bush.

"I can *reach* 'em all," explained Sophie.

"What about your toys?" said Beatrice. She waved her hand at the mountains of toys around the room. Dolls and stuffed animals and blocks and puzzle pieces were all heaped in piles. "At least let me help you organize those."

"No! Don't touch 'em!" shrieked Sophie.

She slid off the bed in a crashing heap and stumbled over to her toys. "I like 'em all over the place 'cause I can *roll* in 'em!"

She and grumpy Mrs. Cow began rolling in the toys.

Beatrice shut her eyes and took a deep breath. She remembered her list of *Things To Do When I Feel Like Exploding*. She had written it yesterday.

This was the list:

1. Don't say anything (note: things said before exploding can be mean and unprofessional)

2. Count to ten (note: I do not find this very effective. Add to list of Things Supposed to Work Which Do Not)

3. Imagine a peaceful, lovely, perfectly organized something (like my room or my lists or making lists in my room)

4. Imagine actually exploding (very messy)
5. Growl to myself
6. Add to my Things That Are Frustrating *list*
7. Take Edison for a walk (fresh air + exercise = calm)

"*Rrrrrrr…*" growled Beatrice quietly, trying out number five. It helped a little.

She walked quickly out of Sophie's room, shut the door on the mess and went across to her own room. She sat at her desk and opened a drawer. She got out her list of *Things That Are Frustrating*.

She found the end of the list.

216. Messy movers

Then she wrote:

217. Sophie's hopelessly messy new room

She thought a bit more, then wrote:

218. Sophie's hair (but she can't help it)

She flipped back through many pages to the beginning of the list.

"This is becoming my longest list ever," she said to her perfect room.

Chapter Three

Beatrice went to find Edison.

She had named their dog after Thomas Edison, the great inventor. He was on Beatrice's list of *Highly Successful, Very Professional People Who Have Done Great Things.*

Her family also had a goldfish. Sophie had named him Super-Pig. Beatrice liked to think Sophie named him Super-Pig because he ate a lot, but she wasn't sure.

"Edison!" she called. "Time for walkies!"

Beatrice walked Edison three times a day. She had read every puppy book in the library. They all said responsible dog owners should walk their dogs at least twice a day. So Beatrice figured that three walks a day would make her the best pet owner she could be.

Beatrice looked for Edison in the downstairs mess.

"Edison!" she called louder. "*Walk!*"

Edison was a big, lazy, shaggy brown dog. He had sleepy eyes and a very big, very drooly mouth. He dearly loved sleeping, especially in sunbeams. Napping, resting and bedtime were three of his favorite activities. He dreaded walks.

"Edison!" yelled Beatrice.

There was no answer. No sound of heavy paws padding down the hall.

"Probably hiding again," she said. Edison usually "hid" by shoving his head under a bed or a sofa.

"Mom, have you seen Edison? I can't find him in all this *mess*."

Her mother was lying on the couch. She looked up from the book she was reading.

"Oh, he's around here somewhere," she said. "Eddie! Ed!"

When he heard the voice of his friend who gave him treats, Edison came lurching up the stairs.

He stopped when he saw Beatrice with the leash in her hand.

He turned and tried to bolt back downstairs, but she caught him around his middle and hauled him back. She wrestled him over to the door.

"You silly dog!" Beatrice said cheerfully. She clipped the leash to Edison's collar. "You always pretend you don't want to go."

Beatrice gave a brisk tug on the leash. Edison sat down heavily, looking back with pleading eyes toward his treat-giving friend. Beatrice went behind him and pushed him. She pushed and pulled him out the door.

"We'll be back soon, Mom," Beatrice panted. "And then I'll help you get this house organized!"

"Mm hmm," said her mom, flipping a page in her book. "Take your time, Bee."

Chapter Four

Beatrice dragged Edison a few steps down the sidewalk. Then he lurched onto the grass and lay on his side.

"Every time, Edison. You do this *every single* time," said Beatrice. She finally reached into her pocket. "Will a treat help?"

Edison's eyes brightened. His ears snapped up. He sat clumsily and waved a big paw. He wolfed the treat down.

Then he shook himself, gobs of drool flying from his mouth.

"I love you, Edison," said Beatrice as they started to walk, "but you are one slobbery dog."

Beatrice looked back at their new house. It was a pretty white house with a blue front door. Through the big living room windows, all she could see were stacks and stacks of boxes. She sighed.

"Just a *short* walk, Edison," she said. "There's lots to do."

They came to the school at the end of the street.

"This will be my school in one month, Edison," Beatrice said. "A brand-new school! I hope grade three is very, very successful."

She felt excited. And nervous.

Beatrice started thinking of a list of *Things to Do to Be Successful in Grade Three*. She had reached number six (*Print business cards*) when she heard a shout behind her. She swung around.

A huge dog was running toward her and Edison from across the school field.

A huge dog with nobody holding the other end of the leash.

The dog's tongue flopped and bobbed out the side of its mouth.

Two girls ran after the dog, but they were much slower than he was.

"Peewee! Come! Stop! Stay! Sit! BAD DOG!" one of the girls yelled.

Edison's ears perked up. For once, Beatrice didn't have to tug his leash to get him going. He took off running toward the other dog.

"Wait! Edison, no, wrong way, WRONG WAY!" yelled Beatrice.

Edison ran straight at the wild, monster-sized dog.

"Other way, *other way*!" Beatrice said. She used both hands to hold on to the leash. Edison pulled and dragged Beatrice along with him. She slipped and skidded in the grass.

This is highly unprofessional, she thought. She gritted her teeth as she bumped along.

The two dogs met in a joyful crash. They rolled and wrestled and tumbled together. Then they flopped down on the grass, panting and wagging their tails. Somehow, Beatrice had kept hold of Edison's leash. She flopped down on the grass beside the dogs.

The big dog turned and licked Beatrice's face with his dripping tongue.

"Ugh, *more* dog drool," Beatrice said. But she petted his huge head.

Beatrice had green grass stains on her knees. Her favorite purple shirt was torn and spattered with dog drool. Her face was red and hot. Strands of hair had escaped her smooth ponytail and stuck to her sweaty face.

She turned to the two girls who ran up.

"Sorry, *sorry*!" said the smaller girl, reaching to help Beatrice to her feet. "Are you okay?"

"I'm fine, thank you," said Beatrice with dignity. She smoothed her rumpled shirt.

Beatrice noticed that the smaller girl had perfectly straight black hair.

I wonder how many times she brushes it every night? she thought. The girl smiled brightly.

"Peewee's so strong! He saw your dog, gave one big tug and he was gone!"

"Wow, these two sure have made friends," said the blond girl. She smiled and scratched Edison behind the ears. "Aww! He's so cute."

Beatrice looked at Edison. He was panting. His tongue was hanging out. He was slobbering all over the place.

Cute? We are both total messes, Beatrice thought.

"I'm Sue," said the blond girl. She had a round face and big, friendly blue eyes.

"I'm Jill," said the dark-haired girl. "And it looks like you've met Peewee." Jill giggled.

Beatrice smiled. The girls might not be perfect pet owners, but they seemed nice.

"I'm Beatrice. That's our dog, Edison. We just moved into the house on the corner."

"Hey! We're almost next-door neighbors!" said Sue. "I live one house away!"

"I live over there, across the field," said Jill.

"Do you both go to this school?" asked Beatrice. It would be wonderful to have a few friends before she even started school. That would be very successful indeed.

"Yep. We're both going into grade three," said Jill. "How about you?"

"Same," said Beatrice happily.

Peewee and Edison got up and shook themselves.

"Well, I guess we should get going," said Sue. "I'm starving."

"And I have tennis lessons," said Jill.

"Hey," said Beatrice, "why don't you both come over to our house later? Maybe three o'clock? We'll be all unpacked and perfectly organized by then."

She got a nervous, sinking feeling as she said this.

"Okay." Jill nodded happily, her black hair bobbing. "See you then!"

"Great!" said Sue, grabbing Peewee's leash. "See you later, Bee!"

Beatrice watched them walk away. Jill did two perfect cartwheels in the field.

Beatrice, she said automatically to herself. *My name is Beatrice.*

But her eye didn't twitch, and she didn't feel much like exploding. She liked those girls.

On her first walk in her brand-new neighborhood, she had almost made two new friends.

How successful was that?

Chapter Five

"Mom!" Beatrice yelled as she banged the door.

She quickly tucked her shoes side by side in the closet. She unclipped Edison from his leash. He slunk over to a sunbeam and flopped on his side with a huge sigh.

"*Mom!*"

Her mother struggled up from the couch.

"Mmmph, I'm up, I'm *up...*" she mumbled.

"Hiya, Bee," said Sophie, who was lying on the living room floor. She was drawing some fish with huge googly eyes on a big piece of paper. Beatrice could see pink, green and blue marker smudges on the floor.

Beatrice took a deep breath.

"Mom, have you unpacked *anything*? What have you been doing?"

Her mother yawned and tried to smooth her frizzy hair.

"Oh, I must have dozed off. Sophie, what a beautiful picture!"

Sophie stopped coloring and leaned back to look at her art.

"Yep, Super-Pig sure is beeyootiful," she agreed, pointing with a grubby finger at a blue fish. "An' them's his fishy friends!" She leaned over and kissed the pink-and-green fish.

Beatrice ran over to her mother. She put her hands on her mother's shoulders. She looked into her face. She spoke slowly.

"Mom, listen to me. I met some girls who might be in my grade-three class! I invited them over to our *perfectly organized* and *unpacked* house at three o'clock! *Three!*"

She pointed to the clock. It was almost noon.

"At three?" said her Mom. "*Today?*"

"Today," wailed Beatrice.

Her mother swallowed.

"We have to unpack this whole house in three hours?" she whispered. "I thought we could do it slowly. A few boxes each day for a couple of weeks..."

"Well, change of plans!" Beatrice said frantically. "We have to do a few boxes each *minute* for a couple of *hours*! Please, Mom!"

Her mother nodded bravely. "Okay, Bee. This seems really important to y—"

"Yes, yes," Beatrice interrupted impatiently. "Thanks, Mom, but there's no time for chitchat! Where's Dad? Is he back from the hardware store?"

"He's in the basement. Unpacking. I'm sure he's unpacking." Beatrice's mother trotted over to the basement stairs.

"Honey, you're unpacking *lots and lots* of things, aren't you?" she called. "Because you-know-who is coming right down!"

Beatrice ran down the stairs. Her father was sitting in a chair with his feet up on a pile of boxes. He had an old book in his hand.

"My high-school yearbook," he explained to Beatrice with a smile. "Funny the things you find when you move house."

"Hilarious," said Beatrice. "Look, Dad, we have to hurry and unpack.

By three o'clock! We have company coming, and the house has to be *spotless*!"

"By three? But there's a baseball game that I—"

Her father stopped talking when he saw Beatrice's face.

He sighed, got to his feet and turned to the boxes.

"Unpacking. Right. I'm on it," he said.

Chapter Six

Beatrice's whole family worked.

Sophie threw down her markers. One skidded a long streak of blue across the floor. "I'll help you make the house *purvect* for your friends, Bee!" she said.

"Thanks, Sophie," Beatrice said. She gave her sister a quick hug, then gathered up the markers. She licked her finger and scrubbed at the blue streak on the floor. It wouldn't come out.

"*Rrrrrrr,*" growled Beatrice softly.

"Mrs. Cow says she hates messed-uppedness too," Sophie said. "It makes her even *more* crabbier."

Beatrice looked over at the grumpy doll, surprised.

Well, thank you, Mrs. Cow, she thought.

Beatrice shooed her mom and Sophie into the kitchen and took charge of the living room.

Soon she had the whole room unpacked and put away. She checked things off her list (which she had written quickly but neatly). It was titled *Unpacking the Whole House in Three Hours.* She flipped to the page for the living room.

1. Books organized

Check.

2. Pictures hung perfectly straight

Check.

3. Plants watered

Check.

4. Cushions plumped

Check.

Time check? According to Beatrice's timetable (stapled to the list), the living

room should be finished by 1:00 PM. It was 12:57. Check.

She was even three minutes early. Excellent.

Beatrice ran into the kitchen.

Her mother and sister were sitting at the kitchen table. They were eating cookies and drinking milk. They both jumped up when they saw Beatrice.

"Just taking a tiny break, Bee," her mother said quickly. "We've done that whole shelf!" She pointed to a small shelf above the kitchen counter. Cookbooks of all shapes and sizes were piled on the shelf. No order. No organization.

Beatrice put her hand up to her left eyelid to stop it from twitching.

"Okay, that *one shelf* looks fine," she said. "Now quickly, quickly, let's get everything else put away. Everything!"

Sophie looked at the cookie in her hand, sighed and dropped it in her milk.

"I put'n my cookie away, Bee!" she said. "But I not sure it can swim." She peered down into the sludgy glass. "Nope."

"Hurry, people, hurry!" pleaded Beatrice, neatly opening a box. "Check the time! It's 1:04 PM! The kitchen should have been done *four minutes* ago! Go, go, GO!"

Her mother hummed while she pulled pots and pans out of a box. She shoved them into a cupboard in a tangled heap. Sophie dumped a box full of plastic containers, opened a cabinet and chucked them inside. She slammed the door quickly on an avalanche of plastic. Beatrice followed Sophie and her mother, fixing, stacking and organizing.

When she turned around, Sophie was eating another cookie and whispering to Super-Pig.

"Hey, Bee," Sophie said through a mouthful of cookie, "I told Super-Pig to clean up his fishy home too." Cookie crumbs flew through the air at this announcement.

"Great. The more—uh—fins, the better," said Beatrice, grabbing the broom.

When the kitchen was finished (late, at 1:49 PM), Beatrice stacked the empty boxes in the garage. She ran down to the basement.

Her father had the baseball game on. He was unpacking slowly as he watched.

"Hi, Bee. You're jus—whoa!" he yelled, his eyes on the television. "It's a hit! That ball is going, going, GONE! Home run!"

He held up his hand for a high five. But it hung in the air. He looked over. Beatrice had her hands on her hips.

"We are *way* behind schedule, Dad," Beatrice said, her eye twitching. "Less home runs, more hard *work*!"

"Got it. Right. Unpacking," her dad said, one eye on the game.

When the basement was finished, her father flopped down on the couch.

"Whew, that was—"

"Time check?" said Beatrice.

Her father looked at his watch. "It's two fifteen," he said.

"WHAT? It's two fifteen *already*?" She pulled her father to his feet. "Hurry—upstairs, NOW!"

"Your friends aren't going to be wandering through all the bedrooms," grumbled her father.

"I promised them a perfectly unpacked house," said Beatrice. "How would I look if they came and the house wasn't perfect? *Unprofessional.* That's how I'd look."

They ran through the living room. Mom and Sophie were reading a picture book on the couch. Her mom looked up.

"Bee, this room looks grea—"

"No time, no time! Everybody, upstairs to the bedrooms! Come on, people, MOVE!" The whole family scrambled up the stairs.

"This is *fun*," giggled Sophie.

"Yeah, it's a real party," muttered her mother.

"Okay," panted Beatrice. "My room is perfect. Sophie's room is"—she swallowed—"how she likes it (and we'll keep that door *closed*). So we only need to do one bedroom and the bathrooms."

"Aye aye, captain," joked her mother, but Beatrice was already down the hall.

They worked quickly, unpacking, organizing and tidying. They threw the empty boxes into the hallway.

Beatrice called out the time every five minutes.

"It's 2:40 PM! Hurry up, hurry up!"

"We're at 2:45 PM! Work, people, work!"

"Now it's 2:50 PM! Ten minutes! Ten minutes left!"

At 2:54 PM the doorbell rang. Edison began barking.

Beatrice looked up wildly.

"What was that? Was that the doorbell?" she shrieked.

"Yep," said her father. "Calm down. They're just a little early. No big deal. We're almost done here."

"They're SIX MINUTES early!" Beatrice yelled. "And *almost* isn't *perfect*!"

She looked at the hallway, which was covered in empty boxes. There was no time to get them all down into the garage.

Beatrice didn't feel like exploding. She was too tired to explode.

She felt like crying.

Sophie ran over and opened the door to her room. "Quick, everboddy! *We'll* chuck all 'em boxes in here," she said, "and *you* go get the door, Bee!"

"Thanks, Sophie!" said Beatrice.

She ran down the stairs, Edison at her heels.

She took a deep breath, smoothed her hair and opened the door.

Chapter Seven

"Hi, Bee!" said Jill. Sue was just behind her, eating a popsicle.

"Hi Jill! Hi Sue! Come on in."

"Hiya, Bee!" said Sue. She came in and kicked off her sandals. They landed in a messy heap. Beatrice itched to tidy them, but that would possibly not be polite.

"Actually," said Beatrice, "my name is Beatrice. Just so you know."

"That's just so *long*," sighed Sue. "I never go by Susannah. I can't even remember how to *spell* it half the time. So I'm just Sue."

"I think Bee is totally cute," said Jill. "Like the letter. Or a fuzzy little bumblebee."

Beatrice smiled.

Maybe Bee wasn't so bad.

"Well," she said, "come in. We finished unpacking a *long* time ago. Yep, we're a pretty organized family," she said nervously. "Every last box put away."

Edison snorted and rolled onto his back, belly up to the sunbeam.

"Eddie!" cried Sue, rushing over to Edison. "How ya doing, buddy?" Edison's tail thumped while Sue rubbed his belly. Dog hair danced in the sunbeam, and a trickle of drool slid out the side of his mouth.

Beatrice's mother and father plodded down the stairs. They looked very, very tired.

Beatrice introduced them to Sue and Jill.

"Who wants cookies?" Beatrice's mom said.

"Oh, *yes, please*," said Sue. "I'm *so* hungry."

Over cookies and milk, the girls talked.

"We have three cats, Peewee and a hamster," said Sue. "I love animals. And food," she said, reaching for another cookie. "I love food."

"I play piano and tennis," said Jill. "And I've just started swimming lessons and gymnastics!"

Beatrice would have liked to look professional in front of her new friends.

But they had just moved, and she wasn't in any lessons at all.

That's going to change, thought Beatrice, making a quick mental list of *All the Many Activities I Plan to Do*. In the blink of an eye, she got from one (*Art*) to twelve (*Cliff diving*).

"I plan to do *lots* of activities," said Beatrice. "But because of the move, I mainly do puzzles, make lists and organize things," she blurted.

"Cool," said Sue.

"This house *is* very organized and tidy," said Jill, looking around.

"It's way cleaner than our house," said Sue. "I have three brothers who mess the place up. Actually, come to think of it, I'm the messiest of the bunch."

"My twin brother is super neat. Annoyingly neat," said Jill.

"Hey, can we see your room?" asked Sue.

"Sure!" Beatrice jumped up. She was very confident about her room.

The girls went upstairs. Beatrice threw open the door to her room.

"Wow. Nice!" said Sue. She walked into the room and flopped on the perfect, wrinkle-free bed.

Sue looked up and saw Beatrice's face. She saw her frown and her twitching left eye.

She sprang up.

"Oh, sorry. I probably messed up your quilt," she said. She tried to smooth it but ended up rumpling the cover even more.

"Here, let me help," offered Jill. She pulled at the sheet and knocked over

Beatrice's neat row of stuffed animals. "Whoops!" she said, shoving them back in the wrong order. "There."

Sue and Jill backed away from the rumpled bed.

Beatrice racked her brain for a clean, organized, quiet activity they could all enjoy. She couldn't think of anything!

I should have made a list of Fun, Non-Messy Things to Do on a Perfect Playdate, she thought in a panic. *Now it's going to be a disaster!*

Jill looked across the hallway.

"Hey, whose room is that?" she asked.

"That's my sister Sophie's room," said Beatrice.

"What does that cute sign say?" asked Jill, crossing the hall to Sophie's door. Sue and Beatrice joined her.

"Aww, it's *adorable*," said Sue. "You sure are lucky to have a little sister."

Beatrice smiled. But she felt a little guilty. Sophie was in the top three on her list of *Things That Make My Left Eye Twitch*.

Then Beatrice got an idea.

She knocked on Sophie's door.

"Hey, Sophie, want to meet my new friends?" she called.

The door crashed open. Sophie stood there, smiling. Her hair was sticking up in all directions. She had pulled on a dinosaur costume from two Halloweens ago. The dino jaws sat on top of her tangled hair.

My little sister looks like a little weirdo, thought Beatrice.

The other girls didn't seem to notice.

"Hiya, Sophie! I'm Sue. That's Jill. Cool outfit."

"I hope you're a *plant*-eating dinosaur," said Jill with a smile, pretending to be afraid.

"I'm a bery *friendly* dinosaur. I'm a play-o-saurus! You guys gonna com'n play?" asked Sophie hopefully. She opened the door of her messy room.

Beatrice looked nervously at her new friends.

Jill smiled.

Sue looked amazed.

"Wow!" Sue said. "Check out all the boxes! Let's play hide-and-seek, play-o-saurus!"

They shrieked with laughter playing hide-and-seek in the messy little dinosaur's messy little room.

They toppled boxes.

They slithered through books.

They rolled in toys.

They made a lot of noise.

They made a complete, utter, total mess.

And it was perfect.

Chapter Eight

When the doorbell rang, the girls were laughing so hard they didn't hear it.

"Girls! *Girls!*" called Beatrice's mother. "Jill's brother is here. Jill and Sue have to get going!"

"Coming!" yelled Sue. "Hey, Jilly-Billy, time to go." She crawled out of a big box. Her bouncing, blond curls were a mess. Her round face was red.

Jill threw back the quilt she was hiding under. "Well, *that* was fun!" she giggled.

The three girls ran downstairs, laughing and making plans to play the next day.

Jill's brother was standing outside. He had black, silky short hair combed neatly above his round glasses.

"Yo, bro," called Jill.

"Hiya, Jimbo," said Sue.

"*James*, Sue," said Jill's brother. "For the millionth time, it's *James*. Absolutely not Jimbo. Jimbo isn't even a *name*."

"It's a *nickname*," laughed Sue. "I give nicknames to everybody I like. Right, *Bee*?"

Beatrice smiled.

"Right, Sue."

Beatrice stood on the steps and waved goodbye to her new friends.

She went back inside. The house was very quiet.

She looked around for her family. She found them downstairs on the big couch, cuddled together and watching a movie.

Her mother's book had fallen on the floor, its pages splayed open.

Her father's tools were scattered across the coffee table.

Sophie was eating popcorn and wiping her buttery fingers on her dino legs. A pile of stuffed animals was heaped on the carpet in front of her.

Edison was sleeping on a chair that was already covered in dog hair. He snored happily in a little puddle of drool.

Beatrice frowned. *Hopeless*, she thought. *This family is absolutely—*

Her mother looked up at her and smiled. Her face looked tired. Beatrice remembered how hard they had worked.

"Hi, honey. Did you have fun with your new friends?"

"It was wonderful!" said Beatrice.

"I *liked* Sue and Jilly-Billy!" said Sophie through a mouth full of popcorn.

"Hey, Bee, the funniest part is coming up. Come join us!" said her father. He shifted over and patted the couch. Beatrice cuddled in between her dad and Sophie. Sophie offered Beatrice the popcorn and a dino leg to wipe her fingers on.

While they were laughing at the movie, Beatrice's eyes wandered above the screen. She couldn't help but notice that the picture her father had hung above the TV was not exactly straight. Not straight at all. In fact, it was eye-twitchingly, head-explodingly crooked.

But her left eye did not twitch.

Her head did not explode.

She did not even jump up to fix it. She was happy right where she was, snuggled on the couch, laughing with her family.

Beatrice smiled as she thought of the perfect list to write later.

She would call it *Reasons Why My Hopelessly Messy, Very Disorganized Family is Almost Perfect.*